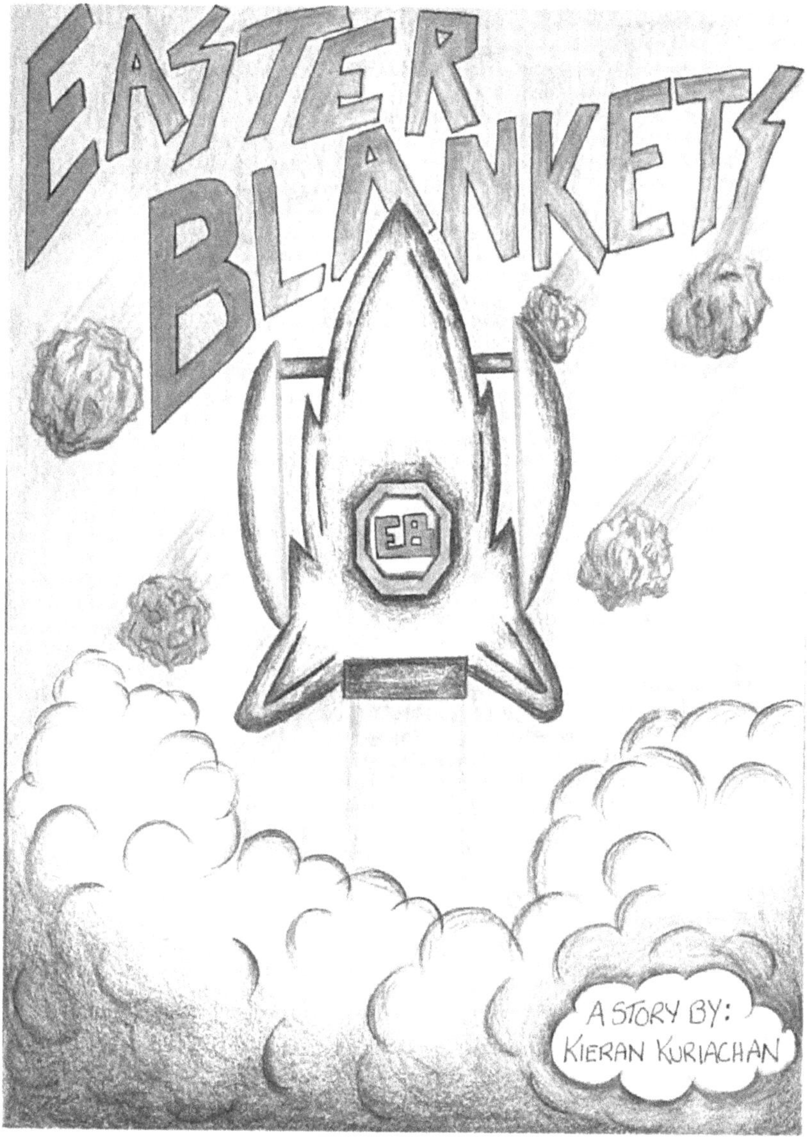
EASTER BLANKETS
EB
A STORY BY:
KIERAN KURIACHAN

Easter Blankets, The Meteoroid Apocalypse
By:
Kieran S. Kuriachan

For my mom Anna, sister Asha, and dad Vikas, along with my friends and supporters Grady, Jayden, Mitchell, Colton, and Brady.

Part I

The Beginning Madness

2095, September 4th

"Come on Lily, it's your first day of eleventh grade. You

have to get up!" yelled Lily's dad.

"Five more minutes dad!" replied Lily.

"Well, okay but you have to get up by yourself because I

have to get to work." her dad impatiently answered.

"I will dad." Said Lily.

"Ok, I have my briefcase, my binder, and my mocha. Let's

get to the airport." her dad mumbled to himself.

BEEP! BEEP! BEEP! "Oh it's 5 minutes all ready! I don't

even think I fell asleep. Hey my clock says 1:00! Oh no I

set it to 5 hours, not 5 minutes. Oh man I have to call

school." exclaimed Lily while grabbing the phone.

Ring,Ring,Ring. "NO ANSWER! I bet mom would know

what to do. I wish she was here right now. But I guess

that's impossible." Lily said sadly while looking at a picture

of herself, her mom, and her dad, not knowing the

calamity that was going to happen next.

Thud. THUD. THUD! The picture in front of her fell and

cracked.

"What's happening?" Lily said looking out the back door.

"Oh my gosh, there is a tsunami!" She ran outside, looked

to her side and saw it. There it was! Coming at her and

she knew she was going to die. It was the end!

The tidal wave was over 500ft high, or at least it looked

that way. It looked like it was going on upwards forever.

There wasn't an ocean near her, where did it come from? She thought to herself. "AHHHHH!" She screamed as she was trapped, under what looked like an ocean, stuck there drowning. Then she felt something stretch behind her neck. The scream turned into a muffle, then everything started to become dark, and she started to drift under the current, losing air, until eventually she became unconscious.

Later...

Lily started to wake up. "What? Where did the wave go? My house is gone. It is very hot. What is that?" Looking at a massive circle.

"OMG that's the sun. It's so close. It is getting closer by the second. Where am I?" Said Lily unsure what was happening, and starting to have a panic attack and starting to hyperventilate. "Hello? Is anyone here?" "Hey there's Hue!" She said with relief, walking up to his

unconscious body. "Hue? Hue? Can you hear me? Come

on! stay with me! No heartbeat. NO!NO!" Lily started to

worry again.

"Lily?" Hue said, gasping for air.

"Oh my gosh you're alive." Lily said, thankfully not having

a heart attack.

"Lily where are we?" Hue asked her.

"I'm not sure. But wherever it is, it's hot." She remarked.

"What's that light Lily?" Hue asked in a worried tone.

"I think it's the sun. But it is getting closer and hotter." Lily

answered.

"We need to find Sarah. She's my little sister. I don't know

where she is and she's only 3. I'm so worried. Can you

please help me find her?" begged Hue.

"I promise I will." guaranteed Lily.

They made their way through Lily's broken house and across her big pond and walked to Hue's house. They couldn't find anything except a bloody arm and a newspaper headline saying The End is Near, and it was dated November 25th, 2097.

"It's been over two years? Exclaimed Hue.

"It's probably a misprint. Anyways, we need to find Sarah. Do you know where she could be?" Lily asked.

 Hue replied, "She is in Arthur's Castle. I know it. It's a fort my dad made for us and is very sturdy. I don't think it fell down because there's massive mountains around it. She and I were going to play there because it was my lunch break at school. So I was biking home and I knew she'd be waiting there for me. As I was biking there, I felt a quake, and then a tidal wave ate me up. I passed out, and I woke up here, but it would've taken a lot of force for the water to get all the way here. Because Hudson's Bay is over ten miles away. So whatever created this was big. Like, even a nuclear bomb couldn't do this, but maybe-" Said Hue getting cut off after going on a rampage of words.

"Hue, where is the fort? I mean Arthur's Castle, where is it?" "Right over there." Said Hue pointing across a lava field that was blowing up lava, not realizing that there was a troublesome path ahead.

"Sorry Hue, but I'm not sure it is possible for anyone to cross that."

"Lily you don't have to go, but my sister needs me, and I am quite positive she is over there. So I guess you can leave, but I'm going to save my sister."

"Ok bye, I hope I see you later." Said Lily. "Just Kidding, I'll come help."

"Thanks Lily. Now let's go."

"Ok we are at the lava, how will we cross it?"exclaimed Lily.

"Well I did do Track and Field so maybe I can run on the grass fast enough to make sure none of the lava hits me." Hue said.

Lily responded with concern, "But Hue, how am I going to get across?"

"No time for planning Lily, it's rising. Just follow me." Said Hue. Then he sprinted as fast as he could across the grass, Lily was right behind him. "We might make it!" Hue said which made him lose his balance. "Lily! Help!" as he slipped. He was still on the grass then Lily tripped over him and knocked him into a small hole in the ground. He hadn't quite fallen in. He held on as tight as he could, Lily grabbed his arm and pulled him up. But it was too late because the lava ahead had risen above the grass and spilled everywhere.

"We have to turn back Hue! We can try to go around the lava by climbing that Plateau." cried Lily.

"Ok Lily, but hurry up, the lava eruption over there is about to get above the grass." shouted Hue.

They ran as fast as they could but still it had risen faster. They were trapped. "Lily I'm sorry. If I wasn't such a wimp and went alone you would have been safe up on the hill."

"No Hue." Lily replied trying to calm Hue.

"Lily It's my fault, even if you-"

"Hue. Look!" Lily screamed cutting off Hue in mid-sentence and getting lifted off the ground into the air. It was a tornado! "AHH!" Screamed Lily. "It's going away, just hold on to me while I hold on to the street lamp!"

"Um, Hue now that it's gone how will we get down?"

"Lily, I think I know a way." Hue said, knowing that the eye of the tornado hasn't come yet. "Hold on as tight as you can Lily!" Hue couldn't hold on anymore so he let go and they went into the air.

"Hue, what now?!" yelled Lily.

Hue replied "The tornado is pushing us to the plateau. Just try to grab the plateau Lily!" They stretched their arms out and grabbed one of the rocks. Lily thought they had a long climb to complete. "Hue, we are somehow gonna climb this thing!"

"No we just have to climb over there and jump into your pond. It will work. Trust me." said Hue.

"Okay." replied Lily and they started climbing near the pond.

Hue hopelessly told Lilly "We can't get to Sarah unless we climb up the plateau, and I don't think we can."

"We will find another way." Lily said about to jump. "On the count of 3, we jump. 1,2," Lily got cut off by Hue.

"Lily when we jump, how do you know that we'll find another way."

"Hue, I promised I would find your sister and I promise I don't break promises." Lily confidently replied.

"Okay Lily, then let's do this." Hue shouted.

"3!" They both said jumping down into the pond. SPLASH!

"Haha, that was fun. Let's do it again." Said Hue jokingly.

"NO WAY! I hate heights and I have a phobia of drowning so this is the opposite of fun for me." complained a very wet Lily.

"Ok well let's look for another way to find Sarah." They looked around and found something that will maybe work. "Hey Lily, what about that. It looks promising."

"Your kidding, right." Lily exclaimed in horror.

"No, I think we can do that." confidently replied Hue.

" So you're telling me you want to go into a dead whale's mouth." Lily said in disgust.

"Sorry I wasn't listening, I was too focused on how you promised me that we would find Sarah." Hue said in a begging voice.

"Fine." They went into the whale mouth and saw that they couldn't reach the blowhole.

"How will we get out of here?" asked Lily.

"Lily, I can lift you up and throw you up to the blowhole. You can grab it and pull yourself out." replied Hue.

"What about you?"

"I think I can figure out a way to the other side." answered Hue.

"Ready and PUSH!"

"I made it through!." Lily yelled delightedly.

"Good, now I'll be there soon." Lily sat there, thinking about what they'll do after they find Hue's sister, and if she will even be at the fort.

She saw a knife cutting through the whale's face, it was Hue. "HUE! You made it through. Where did you get that strong of a knife?"

"I just found it on the ground." answered Hue.

"Oh, well come on. We just need to get past that forest, Hue look, your jacket is on fire!"

"What! Where? Oh, there it is." Hue said before he blew it out. "That dang lava pit." "Anyway, we don't need to go in that forest. Ready?" Hue said, grabbing Lily's hand and stepping on the slippery whale face he cut off and put it in front of him.

"Let's go!" yelled Hue.

"Hue, you're not going for that rocky edge, it's a whale face not a sled!"

"Yes, I am." replied Hue.

He grabbed Lily and pulled her on.

"AHH!" Said Lily, jumping off the whale face. "Your crazy Hue! You could break a limb!"

"Sorry, can't hear you!" He said, almost in mid air. All Lily saw was him go up and then crash into a tree. "Hue. Are you ok?" He didn't answer. "Hue, come on answer me. I need to know you're ok." She looked at his unconscious body and screamed twice then grabbed him by the leg, and dragged him through the forest.

Then she saw a small tree fort and a person inside.

"Sarah! Sarah is that you? I am here with Hue! Sarah?"

Sarah replied "Are you Lily? Hue talks about you all the time." "Oh Sarah. Come here." Lily yelled.

"Hi Ily. Hue has cwush on you." Sarah said to Lily, in a three year old trying to bond sort of way.

"Sarah, is that you?" Said Hue waking up

 "Hue, you're awake."

"Hue, hi Hue" Said Sarah.

 "Lily, you found Sarah." exclaimed Hue.

"Hey, guys. What are those?" Lily asked in a fearful voice.

"Lily, Is that a meteor shower?!" Asked Hue.

"I think so." Lily replied in a worried voice.

"RUN!" yelled Hue.

"Over here! There's a car wash with cars in it." Hue said getting in the car with Lily and Sarah.

"Hue, you can't drive without an adult." exclaimed Lily.

"Lily that law probably doesn't count when you're in a meteor shower!"

"Hue, where are the keys?"

"Awe dose the keys?" Said Sarah, looking across the street at a valet booth.

"Okay, Lily you stay here with Sarah while I go get them."

"Hurry! it looks like one might hit in one to two minutes!"

Hue got out of the car, took one step, and a small meteor hit fifty yards in front of him.

"Okay Hue, it's time to shine. Just run as fast as you can to the valet booth, grab the keys, and get back." He said to himself, as he started running to the booth and looked for the key that looked like the logo on the car. He didn't know what brand it was but in the last few years a new car brand must have become big because more than half of the keys were that company. Half the keys just said Steel Engine with a little drawing of an engine. Then he saw one that matched the color and design as their car so he decided to grab it and ran to the car. "I've got the key. Why isn't it starting?"

"Hue you grabbed the wrong keys, I don't want to sound picky, but quickly get a different key. We don't have much time!" Lily yelled.

He ran back, grabbed one and knew for sure because it had Nevil Shaftnear and the licence plate on the car was NVIL $!. He then ran back, got in the car and drove as fast as he could. "Where are we going Lily?"

"Get to the airport, My dad's a pilot. He can get us somewhere safe." Lily commanded.

They started their long car ride. As soon as they got to the airport, they saw a group of people, some were praying, some crying, and some were singing. But all of them were tearing up. "What's happened here?" Lily asked a man.

She couldn't see his face because his back was turned.

"Lily?" Asked the man.

"Dad!"

"Hey guys, it's my dad! He can fly us somewhere safe."

"Uh sweetheart there is nowhere safe. The world got hit

by an asteroid, it caused a tsunami here and moved us

around the orbit. We now are only thirty million

kilometers away from the sun. Since the asteroid hit us on

an angle so all the heat from the sun went to everybody

else in the world it is overheating. But for some weird

unknown reason all the people in North America are

around the same temperature. All people over eighteen

were notified about it one year before it hit and I ordered

a special protective device for each of us, it can keep you

warm and give you air, food, and water. Once it see's the

weather change to be bad where you are, it will start

working, when the weather is good, it will wait two months and then it will wake you up and stop giving you anything."

"Mr. Jackson, does that mean we have almost been asleep for six months ?" asked Hue.

"Hue, I'm sorry to tell you this but, we've all been asleep for two years. The device stopped our growth too." stated Mr. Jackson.

"Wait, so I'm actually eighteen!" exclaimed Hue.

"Hue, I am in kindwagaten then?" asked Sarah.

"Who are you?" Asked Mr. Jackson

"I'm Sawah and I can count to one hundwed." proudly Sarah stated.

"Wow, that's awesome." Said a young boy that was singing. "I can almost count to one-sousand. I can teach you."

"Ok." Said Sarah, opening the car door and getting out.

"You two don't go out of where we can't see you."

"Ok Hue" Said Sarah

"Mr. Jackson, why are there all the meteors hitting if all

that's happened is we got closer to the sun?"

"What do you mean meteors? You mean the big asteroid

that hit two years ago?"

"Mr. Jackson, we got a meteor shower back at my house.

And tornadoes and climate changes and a whale on land."

"You two had all this happen to you?"

"Yes dad, we did."

"I'll need to tell the Space Agency, and you two stay right

here, I'll be back in a couple hours."

"Where are you going?"

"To Houston" Mr. Jackson said, running over to the singing people, grabbed one, and ran to the plane with him. They got inside and left.

"Well it's just us again Lily."

"Yup, just us."

"Lily, I was wondering if, well we make it through all of this, would you like to-" Hue shyly started asking.

"Hue, shhh. I hear something."

"Lily look, It's Sarah and the other boy running back."

"Hue, I think there trying to say something."

"Lily, Hue. Start the car! Start the car!" Hue started the car and let Sarah and the other boy in.

"Look Hue and Lily. It's like a weird dusty tornado."

"Sarah, that's a sand storm."

"We just have to stay in the car everyone." stated Hue.

"What about all the people outside singing and praying?"

"We need to get them to the inside of the airport." Hue and Lily got out of the car and started telling everyone about the sandstorm. They got inside the airport. But Lily saw a baby in a carrier back where they were outside.

"Hue I need to go do something." She ran outside, got the carrier and started running back. The storm was soon only a few yards away. She got inside and quickly shut the door, and locked it.

"Who's baby is this? Hello?"

"Oh my goodness you saved my baby!" said the lady that was the baby's mom.

"Here you go mam" Lily said handing her the baby.

"Okay Hue, I think it's passed."

"Lily, what I was going to say was, if we make it out alive then maybe we could just, you know, hang out." Hue brought it up again.

"Hue, I can't hear you. I think someone is screaming. Let's go check it out." said Lily.

"Ok Lily." Said Hue, kind of in a frustrated voice. They got to the screaming person.

"What's wrong? Why are you screaming?" Asked Lily.

"My dog ran off and I think that's her." She said turning her head toward a dog body that looked like it was dead.

"Mam, I can feel a heartbeat. I think she might make it."

"Oh thank you young girl, how can I repay you?" asked the dog's owner.

"No need mam, it's ok." Lily said walking away.

"Did you actually feel a heartbeat?" Asked Hue, making sure the owner couldn't hear.

"No, but she looked so upset."

"Lily you lied to that old lady!"

"Yes, I feel so bad but I didn't want to make her more sad"

They said walking away from the dog and the old lady.

There was a loud noise that came from outside.

"Lily, what was that?"

"There is a plane out of control!" Lily screamed.

"It's a huge plane." "It's not slow enough and it could

crash into the west wing of the building."

"Hue, get everyone to evacuate, I need to warn them."

Lily said. She ran outside and got in a plane in front of the

runway.

She took the speaker and said into it.

"Everybody stay calm. Just get outside." Lily got out of

the plane and went to Hue. "Is everyone out?"

"Yes." Said Hue. The plane crashed into the building and made a huge explosion.

"I hope nobody was on the plane."

"Lily, someone would have been piloting the plane." noted Hue.

"I mean I hope it wasn't a passenger plane."

"Yeah, me too." Hue said, as he and Lily walked to the plane crash to see what's going on.

"Lily, help me open the plane door." Hue said, pulling as hard as he could with Lily. They opened it and saw Mr. Jackson's lucky bracelet in the pilot seat and the co-pilot was injured and screaming in agony because a glass shard was stuck in his shoulder.

"Dad?!" Screamed Lily.

"Dad?!" Lily could hardly breath.

"What happened?"

"Mr. Co-pilot guy, Tell me what happened!"

"Lily calm dow-"

"NO! I want to know where my dad is! Sorry, sorry, just I am so worried."

"Lily I am sorry and it's ok to cry and be sad. And who are you anyways?" Hue asked the man.

"I'm Reagan McDonald! I am in a lot of pain because the windshield broke and sliced my shoulder! We were on our way to Houston and the Statue Of Liberty fell and hit the left engine and we tried to glide back to JFK airport! Your dad jumped into the ocean, and I couldn't stop in time and now this has happened!"

"We need another plane, Reagan. We need to tell the Space Agency somehow." Hue said.

"We also need another pilot. I'm just a co-pilot." They looked around for a co-pilot. Reagan looked closely inside Hue's car. "Johnny?" He said.

"Dad!" Johnny said.

"Who is that you're talking to?" Mr. Reagan said.

"I'm Sawah." Sarah answered for Johnny.

"What's in youw shoulder Daddy?" Asked Johnny.

"It's just a little cut. Johnny, why don't you and your new friend come and help me and Hue find a pilot?" Reagan said.

"Ok." They both said

"I heard you're looking for a pilot." Said a man smoking something weird.

"Yeah, and I actually just found a person over there. She is a pilot for sure."

"No he isn't and I can pilot even while I smoke this stuff."

"Ok?" Hue mumbled worriedly to himself.

"What are you smoking?" Mr. McDonald asked.

"I don't know, just bought it from that guy." He said, pointing at a dirty clothed man.

"I'm gonna look for a pilot elsewhere."

"No! You aren't!" The man said, grabbing Reagan's son.

"Let go of him!" Reagan said punching the man in the face. The man fell to the ground, and that made him let go of Johnny. "Come on Johnny, let's look for a pilot." They found a woman who showed them her pilot's license.

"Can you fly to Houston?"

"Yes," The woman said.

"Good, Johnny, you go over to Hue. I'll be back soon. They left to go to Houston.

"Hey, Jolly Johnny." Said the weird smoking man.

"Nobody can protect you now!" He grabbed Johnny by the collar of his shirt.

"Hey, stop it man!" Said Hue.

"No! You stop!" Hue grabbed Johnny and the man punched Hue.

"Haha. Not so tough now!" Hue punched back and the man threw Hue to the ground and beat him up.

"Hey, Sanjay. That's enough. He's just a kid." Said a friend of Sanjay. Sanjay got up and left. Hue had a bloody nose and black eye.

"Hey, Sanjay. You suck at fighting!" Said Hue. Sanjay turned to Hue, dropped whatever he was smoking, and started running at him. Hue got in his car and drove it into Sanjay's leg.

"Ah! Man! I think it's broken!" Sanjay said. Hue smiled.

"HUE!" Lily screamed

"Oh man." Hue said quietly to himself.

"Hue why did you run into him?!"

"Because he gave me this." Hue said, turning his face towards Lily. "Ok, well don't do that!" She said, pulling Hue out of the car. "And you don't beat up people!" She said to Sanjay "Now apologise!"

"Sorry?" Hue said in a confused way. Sanjay just walked away. "Come on Hue, I've got to show you something."

"Okay." Said Hue walking to the part of the airport lounge that wasn't hit.

"Look, it's your dad!" Said Lily.

"Hey Hue." His dad said as they both hugged.

"Dad, you're alive! Where's mom?"

"In Vermont helping out the Space Agency."

"Will I see her soon?"

"Maybe." Said Mr. Hawkins.

"Dad!" Said Sarah running over.

"Oh honey. Hey Sarah." Sarah hugged her dad and he told her where their mom was. "Now let me tell you about this guy." Mr. Hawkins said, opening the door and letting a man in. "Hue, Lily, Meet Mr. Hawkins."

"Who is he dad?"

"I'm your new dad as well." Said the man

"Did mom get remarried?"

"No, I did." Said their father. "I'm gay."

"Oh. That makes sense."

"What does gay mean?" Asked Sarah.

"It's when a man likes a man." replied Hue's dad.

"Oh."

"You guys are already married?" Asked Lily

"Yup."

"Hue, wiwy, you might want to check this out." Said

Johnny pointing to missiles above them coming down.

"There's like, four of them!" Said Hue.

 "Duck and cover everyone, they're about to hit." BOOM!

"Is everyone ok?" Lily said.

"Yes. Where did the missiles come from?" Asked Hue.

"I don't know." Said Lily.

"But look, Reagan's back!"

"Good, that means in a few minutes Johnny will be safe.

"Hue saw Sarah crying on the floor.

"Oh Sarah, you don't need to cry, everyones ok and the

missiles hit over there."

"Hue, wook." She said, looking at Sanjay holding Johnny.

"Hi Hue." Said Sanjay.

"Stop it you disgrace!" Said Hue.

"I'd rather not." Said Sanjay.

"Stop!" Yelled Hue.

"Listen Hue, I'm gonna count down from fifteen and if you don't bring me that girl, Sarah is her name I believe, then little Jolly Johnny, will only have one ear, and six toes."

"No Hue. Doet give her to him, I wiw heaw fine wiff one ear, and I doe need that many toes, even one on each foot is pwetty good." Said Johnny, who sounds like a three year old.

"15, 14, 13 ,12."

"Sanjay you are a stupid idiot who will never have friends, or a wife, or happiness!"

"9, 8, 7, 6, 5."

"You need help! You insane idiot!"

"3,2."

"NO!" Said Hue running and grabbing Johnny and punching Sanjay in the stomach.

"Hue, you've made a grave mistake." Sanjay said, grabbing Hue and pulling him to a car.

"Get in!" Sanjay said with his hand against his face. Hue got in. Sanjay drove to a pond and grabbed some rope.

"What are you doing?" Hue asked. Sanjay put some dishes on Hue's lap and held Hue's face.

"Don't move!" Sanjay said. He tied Hue up and duct taped his mouth shut.

"MMM! MMMMMM!"

"I don't know what you're saying but you are about to suffer. I know you know the feeling of drowning, but will be much, much, worse." Sanjay threw Hue in the lake.

"Goodbye Hue." Sanjay saw a big truck coming to the lake. He saw it was two men and one looked like an older

Hue. Sanjay got in his car about to drive away when the two men hit him.

"What the heck are you doing?" Sanjay yelled at the men. He realized they were Hue's fathers. They were pushing his car into the lake. One of them got out of the car and ran into the lake. He came out with Hue on his shoulder.

"Oh no." Said Sanjay when his buttons to put the window down weren't working. He couldn't open the door. Soon all of the car was underwater. The men untied Hue and woke him up.

"You ok buddy?" Asked Hue's step father.

"I'm good." Hue said.

"I've got to do something." Hue said, grabbing of the axe's that was in the back of the truck. Hue got out of the car and went underwater. They saw him make a hole in Sanjay's car window, it was big enough for Sanjay to fit through, but it was also big enough to pour water into the

car. Hue came out of the water and got in the car.

"Let's get back to the airport then." Hue said.

Sanjay got out of the car.

"Get back here Hue!" Sanjay said, as they drove away.

They got back to the airport.

"Hue, your back!" Lily said running to the car and hugging

him.

"What happened to Sanjay?" Lily asked.

"Oh you don't want to know what happened to that guy."

Hue's step father replied with a snicker.

"Ya." Hue said.

"Come on. Sarah was worried about you." Lily said, taking

Hue to Sarah.

"Hue!" Sarah said, running up to him and hugging him.

"I'm okay." Hue said.

"Umm. Hue what does that plane say?" Sarah asked Lily and Hue, since she couldn't read.

"Hue, it's a US Army and Front Command plane, it looks like a lot of people are on it, or, dog creature things!?" Lily said with a gasp.

"Lily, look. It's a Space Agency plane." Hue said.

"Hue, I can't believe it," Lily said.

"Is that what I think it is." She said again.

"All the planes are landing Lily!" Hue said.

"Hue, look behind us." Lily demanded

"Lily. Is that the president."

Part II
Federal Destruction

September 4th, 2095.

"President, the Secret Service just told me the asteroid

will hit soon. Let's get to the bunker." exclaimed Izic, the

President's assistant.

"Coming Izic. Can you tell Jackson and Karen to pack up.

They are in their rooms." stated the President."Is the first

lady already in the bunker?"

"Yes." replied Izic.

"Ok, I'll go get your kids sir." Izic went down the hall to a

door with a sign that says "NO BOYS!" and walked in.

"Karen?" He asked.

"Hi Izic, I'm all packed." Said a teenage girl dressed in all

goth clothing.

"Ok, then come with me to the bunker. Your father is waiting for us." Izic took Karen to the bunker. He went back up and went into a room. "Hey Jackson." Izic said

"Hi Izic. Look outside." Jackson said in a calm voice somehow. Izic looked outside and saw the tidal wave coming. "Ohh god." Izic said, grabbing Jackson and his suitcases and running to the stairs. "Get down the stairs, quickly!" Izic said, running down the stairs. He got to the bunker.

"Hey Izic, where's Jackson?" The President said. "Oh no. He didn't come down!" SMASH! The wave smashed through the white house windows and the president, the first lady, and the president's daughter Karen all started panicking.

"Maybe he survived. I'll go check." Izic opened the door and gallons of water started coming into the bunker.

"Ahh!" Karen screamed. Jackson was in the water and floated into the bunker, coughing up water. Izic closed the door and locked it. "Are there any towels in the bunker?" Jackson asked. "Oh sweetheart, you're ok!" Said the first lady while all of them except Izic hugged him.

"Ok, we might be here a while."

"Dad, I secretly ordered some special devices to give air and water and a lot of things." said Jackson.

"Good, How many?" asked the President.

"Four. I got the right amount."

"Will I get one?" Izic asked.

"Sorry I didn't plan for five" Jackson said.

Izic realized he was gonna die soon so he decided to start pushing the boy. "Stop!" The first Lady said. The president ran over and punched the guy in the face. He still didn't stop. "I'll kill you!" Izic said. The president tried pulling him off of Jackson. He still held on. Jackson started wheezing from his asthma. "Stop!" The first Lady said again. "Please!" She said again. Jackson passed out. "I just have to get to finish Jackson! Then I'll get your daughter." yelled Izic. Karen screamed while she was crying. The president jumped on to Izic and finally knocked him over. The first Lady grabbed her son and started doing CPR to him. "You fool!" Izic said, grabbing the President and punching him until the president was in so much pain he didn't want to move. Izic ran back, pushed the first Lady out of the way and grabbed Jackson. "Why won't you die!?" Izic screamed trying to choke the boy. "No, please no!" The first Lady said. "Sorry pal!" The President said, taking out his metal phone looking device and hitting Izic as hard as he could two times. Izic let go of Jackson and was almost knocked-out. "If I ever see you again, I'll torture you, and your family!" Izic said as the President took a final swing with his phone and knocked Izic out. The President took all of the devices, gave one to each person and put one on his own neck and Jackson's neck, then he grabbed the door handle. "Ready everyone?" He said. "Yup." Karen and the first Lady both said. He swung open the door and threw Izic out as the water came in.

2 Years later.

"Uh, the devices made it go by fast." Karen said. "What happened?" Jackson asked.

"Well your dad beat-up Izic and saved your life." The first Lady said. Jackson gave his dad a hug, and used his inhaler. "Guy's. Look." Karen said. They looked outside the bunker door. They were on a river floating towards a waterfall. "Dad, what do we do?" The President reached to grab the door handle to close the door, but the door fell off. "Uh guy's, everybody get to the back of the bunker and brace yourselves!" The President grabbed a long stick that was floating by and tried using it as an oar. It didn't work. He saw 2 rocks that were lined up side by side, but the bunker would float through. He put the stick one side on each rock to stop the bunker from going through. "I hope everyone can swim. And I hope the stick doesn't break." He said, jumping out of the bunker and swimming to the shore. The rest followed soon afterward.

"What now?" Karen asked.

"JFK Airport." Jackson said.

"What?" The President and Karen said confused.

"I've done a ton of research, JFK airport's planes are waterproof and even from a wave like that they'll still stay durable. They modified them thirteen years ago." said Jackson.

"So we're gonna walk to New York?" said Karen questioned.

"No, the Washington Dulles International Airport has tons of planes from JFK Airport, I'm sure all of them survived as well." Jackson said.

"Then let's get going." The first Lady said. They started walking in the direction of the airport. Hours later they still hadn't reached their destination. "Mom, I'm tired of walking!" Karen said.

"Honey, we're almost there." The first Lady said.

"Ok." She said.

"Guys. Look, it's our private jet!" Jackson said. "It's in the engineering building. And we hired engineers from JFK airport, what are the chances?" The First Lady said.

"Let's go over there." Jackson said. They changed their direction and headed to the building. "Finally, we're here. My legs are killing me." "I'll go in, and. Wait, Who's gonna pilot?" The President asked.

"Just go inside." The first Lady said. The President went inside. He saw a weird shadow pass him in the hallways. "Hello?" He asked. "Who's there." He looked behind him at the corner of the hallway and saw long skinny fingers grabbing the edge of the wall.

"HHHHELLO." The president heard from the body of the fingers. "Hello?" The president said back, scared and shivering. "Remember me?" Said a bald, metallic skinned, dark grey, skinny creature coming around the corner. The president ran as fast as he could. The thing caught up to him and grabbed him and said "It's me, Izic. The Space Agency hired me. I was the test launch to outer space. To see if we could live on another planet after this one becomes a fiery death rock. The agency didn't help me. They saw the ship blow up. But it wasn't anything to them. They just thought that I was a test monkey. You did too. That's why I need you now. I need you to die. Then maybe someone will care about me!"

"NO,NO!" The president said.

"Goodbye Mr. President." Izic wrapped his long skinny arms around the president's head, and then he put the tips of his finger in the president's ears to use a special power. The president stopped breathing. The first Lady and Jackson and Karen were hiding behind the wall.

"Alright kids we have to be quiet." She whispered to them in a soft voice. ACHOO! "KAREN! You blow our cover!" Jackson said. Izic walked around the corner. "Hello children."

"AHHHH!" They both said staring at the hideous being.

"Jackson, oh Jackson. I hate you so much".

The president started to breathe again.

"I've got an idea. Mr. President, let me have Jackson, and

I'll let you go." said Izic.

"AHH!" Jackson yelled.

"Do it!" Izic said once again. The first Lady saw a wrench

and swung as hard as she could at him.

"No!" Izic said.

"Not metal." It hit him in the stomach. They heard a

sizzling sound! "Ouch! I'll be back!" Izic said, dropping the

President on the ground and running away. "He was so

fast it looked like he just faded away." Karen said.

"Everyone. I guess we got off on the wrong foot. I'm Izic."

They heard the speakers. "I crashed in a spaceship a few

years ago. Right into an asteroid. But luckily there were

green organisms that looked like shiny rocks. Some of me

touched them and we merged. Half a year later the

asteroid hit a planet. The planet was Earth. I've been

looking for someone ever since I landed in the Pacific

Ocean. I actually was gonna look for them since they

almost let me drown. I was gonna look for them when I

ran up the stairs and out the window and I got in the car

and drove to Houston. But I forgot about it when The

Space Agency was hiring someone who could take a risk.

Then as soon I came back to Earth I realized something,

maybe people will finally know who I am if I killed their

leader. But of course you have found metal. But me and

my friends will get you soon. There are my friends." All of

them looked out the window and saw hundreds of ships

hitting the surface of the Earth with thousands of things

coming out of each one. They heard the speaker start

talking again. "I bet you thought that the other organisms wouldn't come to life either. Well you thought wrong. But they didn't only come alive. They also gained intelligence. They built all those ships. They made future ranmintion and invisible shields. Let's just see how powerful your puny little metal is now."

"Come on guys! Let's get in the plane!" They ran in the plane. They saw a guy sitting there in the pilot seat.

"Oh, hello Mr. President, your plane has been ready for a while I was just waiting in here because, well my house is destroyed. Everyone sit, I'll fly us wherever you want to go." The pilot said in a spanish accent. They sat there for about a minute. "Well, where do you want to go?"

"New York City." The president said. All the aliens were surrounding the plane, but as soon as one touched, because the plane was made from metal, they made a loud squealing noise as the aliens would burn.

DDDDRRRR! They took off and touched some of the

aliens. Karen and Jackson saw the aliens melt until they

were just a burn mark on the concrete. "We made it!" The

first Lady said.

"I thought I saw more of them, and didn't Izic say they

made futuristic weapons." said the President.

"It's probably fine."

"But there are still some of them at the building." The

president said, going into the captains box. The plane

turned around and they ran over all the aliens that were

still alive. "Woo!Hoo!" The president said, coming out of

the captains box. Izic was the only alien left there, but his

arm hit the plane and burned off.

"I'll get you!" Izic screamed at the plane, but it was too far

up for them to hear him.

"Hey dad, what's that big glowing circle?" Jackson asked.

"Um, I think that's the sun." The president said.

"But that's way bigger than the sun looks like from Earth." Karen said. "Hey what's that little circle in the distance?"

"I think that the little circle is Venus and it's close because we moved closer to the sun from the asteroid." The first Lady said.

"Mom is probably right."

"Ya, but the Earth rotates, it wouldn't go straight, to the sun."

"Except if the asteroid hit it hard enough, then the impact from the beginning hit it hard enough, but still why isn't it hotter, and why isn't the Earth brighter?" The president answered and asked.

"Well folks it was 12:00 PM when the asteroid hit, so the moon was facing Asia and it was night there. And it took maybe a year and 12:00 hours to get close enough that it would burn you. And the moon was facing us and it was night here. The asteroid hit the Pacific Ocean and flooded North America but it hit right on the Mariana Trench and got all the water to flood out of the ocean, but the Mariana Trench isn't too deep for that to happen, and that means after it hit it could have reached the bottom. And the light side of the moon was blocking the sun because after it got out of the way, we would have been on the other side of the Earth, and the sun wouldn't have faced us. With the asteroid in the middle of the ocean when the sun started facing us another piece of the asteroid might have hit the Antarctica side of the Pacific and launched cold water in the area where the first asteroid hit, filling up all the water where the primary asteroid hit. But another piece landed in the Pacific

Ocean, which caused a 2nd wave to go across North America. But it was cold water that normally would have frozen you to death, but thanks to the closeness of the sun we were fine. From all the waves North America shifted 600 Kilometers north. But it's not snowing because the sun melts the snow quickly. So that is all the explanation we've got." Said William Anderson on a TV on the Live Hetamont News Channel.

"Well that pretty much explains it." The first Lady said.

"Mom! Dad! Look!" They said looking out the window at 4 missiles with an army plane launching them. They saw the statue of liberty in front of them. It had marks from getting hit by a plane wing. "Oh My God!" The president said. The plane started turning around. "Let's get some sleep." Karen said. "Ok but we only have 15 minutes."

"Wait, Look out this telescope." They all saw a huge

asteroid hit Mars. "Oh boy. We have to land." The president said watching the plane crash into the airport, as soon another one flew off. "Watch out!" They watched as the army ship launched their missiles at the airport.

"Just land in like, 10 minutes." The president said.

"Is that not a Space Agency aircraft?" The First Lady said, looking at a Space Agency aircraft.

"We should land now." Jackson said.

"Does that plane have more of the aliens on it?" The First Lady asked.

"I guess we'll have to find out." The president responded, unknowingly of what might happen to them if Izic was still alive, and what might happen to everybody else.

Part lll

Mission Mayhem

Sept 4th, 2095.

"Captain Duke. The Space Agency's seeing the heat signature entering our atmosphere." Said a man wearing camo who looked like a navy seal.

"Just say asteroid, you don't look any smarter than I do by using fancy words like signature."

"Sorry Captain, but signature is only nine letters."

"It's fine Kent, now how much damage do you think it will do?"

"I'll call The Space Agency and see." Kent went to the phone and dialed a number into it.

"Hi, um the asteroid won't do much, right." Kent stopped talking and listened.

"Oh my gosh! You must be kidding!" Kent put down the phone and turned to Captain Duke.

"Sorry, but um. Well just hope you didn't want all your bones to be located in the proper position."

"Why?" They both looked out the window and just saw one hint of the massive asteroid as it hit the ocean and created a huge tidal wave.

"That's why." Duke answered.

Two scientists, (one boy and one girl), came into the room and put little metal chips on the back of their necks.

"What are you doing?"

"These special devices will help you stay alive." The female scientists said. "See you in two years." The male scientist said as the windows broke and the tsunami crashed into the building. "What do you mean two years!?" Captain Duke said, but right as the female scientist was going to answer, the wave hit them.

2 years later…

"Captain Duke? Where are you?" Said Kent.

"Hey your up now. I've been up for hours." said the female scientist.

"Here's Captain Duck or whatever."

"Captain Duke?" Kent said as he woke Captain Duke up.

"Liam? Liam? Come on wake up" She said to the male scientist, trying to wake him up.

"Um, you might want to look at the back of his neck." The female scientist flipped over Liam. She saw that his device had come off of his neck.

"How did it fall off?" The scientist said, crying over Liam's body.

"It looks like he tore it off." Caption Duke said, as Kent picked up Liam's hand and showed the scientist Liam's device was in his own hand.

"I think someone else tore it off." Duke stated.

"Why's that?" Kent asked.

"Because, someone wrote something on his other hand, and it says DIZI in marker, his name isn't DIZI."

"Let's get to white house, the president is probably still in his bunker."

"Well I guess you could say he is in his bunker, because he is, but not in the white house."

"What do you mean?"

"Look at the white house cameras, him and his family are flowing down that river that the tsunami made toward that- OH NO! They're gonna fall down the waterfall."

"Don't worry, they grabbed that log and locked it with two rocks. And now they're going to shore."

"Oh no, I don't know if they all got off in time. Can you see if they're behind that rock?"

"Well let's just hope so." The female scientist said, walking to the window, watching as the bunker flipped over the log and fell off the cliff, going down, down, down, until nobody could see it.

"Is Liam ok?"

"No, he dried up, It must have been taken off not long ago. His heart monitor was just straight lines. He is gone, for sure. And before you ask, yes I'm ok, even though he was my co-worker, and best friend, I can't sulk about it

when it'll be the end of the world soon."

"Well, let's make his death worth it. Follow me." Captain

Duke said as they walked down the hall.

"Look at this screen." The captain said, as they looked at

the screen.

"Is that Mars? It looks like it's a burnt piece of bacon."

"Wait, Captain Duke, The system must be broken because

this is supposed to be the camera in Berlin?" Kent said.

"Wait, nothings broken, that's the Reichstag Building."

The female scientist said.

"Good, you figured that out. Maybe you can figure out

what that is." The captain said, pointing out the broken

window at a strange glowing ball that was massive.

"Please don't tell me that's the sun."

"Well if I didn't, I'd be lying." Captain Duke said.

"Pinch me." Said Kent, as he passed out.

"Oh my gosh!" The female scientist said as Captain Duke caught him before his head hit the ground.

"How did he pass out? I know it is surprising that the sun is so huge, but he is a new army recruit, so why'd he pass out so easily?"

"Because of that." The captain said, while they both saw hundreds of massive ships landing on the ground. They also saw thousands of aliens coming out of them, some wearing strange armour with weapons, others not having anything. "Oh no, all the high tech ones are coming for us, and all the normal ones are going the other way!"

!BOOM! A blue laser exploded the wall and shot through the broken window. "RUN!" The female scientist jumped out of the window falling past the first floor and hitting the dumpster, then Captain Duke did the same thing with unconscious Kent on his shoulder. They started running.

Captain Duke looked back, he saw a massive bomb hit the building they were in. "GO! GO! GO!" He said, as the female scientist saw something fly about fifty meters above them get ahead of them about to hit the ground. "Stop moving! That thing could be a bomb." She said. It hit the ground and started making a massive force field around them and the aliens.

"Oh NO!" They both said, knowing they were gonna be trapped with the beasts. The aliens, thousands of them, all stopped as they saw Captain Duke and the female scientist both backed up against the force field wall, while Kent started to wake up. "Oh dear god!" Kent said as he opened his eyes, and got his back up against the wall too, holding out a weapon looking like a gun.

"bzswaMNaDzjNza.ajznkjakjaWJQSASK!" One of the aliens said, which made all the aliens back up.

"I guess they speak gibberish." The female scientist said.

"Maybe Kent can translate it. You know, you still haven't given me your name." Captain Duke said to the female scientist.

"Rose." She answered.

"Cool, now let's focus on the fact that we're about to get killed by extra terrestrial fishes with massive guns and gadgets!" Kent yelled. Kent thought of something he had done earlier that day, well, 2 years ago technically.

"Follow me." He said, running around the edge of the force field. They were only 70 meters away from the mob of aliens, when Kent pointed out that behind some of the aliens there was a shovel.

"It's just a shovel Kent." Duke said.

"But shovels dig." Kent said.

"Yep, that's what shovels do. What about it." Said Duke.

"Duke, Rose, We can dig with that shovel."

"Yes Kent, I think everyone can dig with a shovel. Now get to the point!" Duke said.

"If we get the shovel, we can dig out of the weird bubble thing by going underneath."

"How do we get the shovel Kent?"

"Well we, you know, maybe we can, only if we could, I have no idea." Kent said, trying to think of an answer.

"I think I know how to get the shovel, but not by getting through all the aliens to the shovel, we can get the aliens to give it to us, and to do that we can pretend like we want nothing to do with it, but then they'll think it's dangerous to us and throw it at one of us."

"But what happens to the person they throw it at."

"Well, are you guys able to catch it?" Rose asked

"Yes, we probably could." they both said.

"Well then wish me good luck." Rose said, screaming about how much she doesn't like the shovel, trying to get the aliens' attention. One of them heard her, and put a strange translating device against his ear, then he yelled in the aliens' language

"HVUFVIYFHGFUGHIHVJB!!"

"I hope that means that they'll throw it at me, you guys ready?"

"Yes."

"Uh huh." Kent said. One of the aliens grabbed the shovel, and threw it. The shovel was in the air coming at her. Both the men came running in front of her, and they caught it. "Let's dig!" Duke said, but Kent got distracted, and dropped the weapon that scared the aliens, which made the aliens less scared, and one of them took a couple steps forward, soon all of them were running at them. Duke and Kent impaled the shovel through the ground, and made a small hole, but it wasn't deep enough for them to get out. Rose looked backwards.

"Oh, um guys, I don't want you to look backwards, but please hurry up!" She said.

"Why?" Duke said looking back.

"Oh God! Quickly Kent!!" They pulled the shovel out of the ground, It was just big enough to fit Rose, she climbed through. "Come on now!" They put it back in the ground and pulled. Kent climbed through, getting squished. Duke was right behind him and he was almost out as an alien grabbed his foot. Kent grabbed Duke's hand, so did Rose. One of the aliens that still hadn't moved forwards, had a weird rifle looking thing pointed at Duke's head, but the alien was far, so they hoped he would miss. They pulled

him out right as the alien pulled back the trigger.

"Come on!" Duke said they followed him as the aliens

struggled to get out but were too big to fit through. He

walked them to a military garage, that's where he showed

them something.

"I call this thing the ThunderRover!" He said, as they all

looked at something that almost looked like a massive

mars rover dune buggy, but it was cool, and very strong.

The aliens fit through the hole and started running to

them. They got in and started driving.

"Ya know, instead of having a bumper sticker with your

kids math achievement on it, if you have spikes made out

of highly-heated tungsten, you'd think that you'd scare

almost anything off, yet look behind us." Kent said, as

they all saw thousands of laser bullets and aliens flying by them.

"You guys know the movie Jumanji? Well why don't we do what they did." Kent said.

"What's Jumanji?" Duke said.

"It's a movie from the 2010's and it was a hit, and I mean when in one scene they drive off a cliff."

"There's no cliff here!" Duke said back.

"We could jump off of that broken overpass onto the building where they can't get us."

"That won't work."

"I don't care!" Kent said jumping into the front seat and turning the wheel.

"AHH!" They said as they went into the air, through the building and almost falling off of the side. They were stuck in the 11th floor of a building, with the Aliens still following them, and crawling up the building.

"What do we do?!"

"Run up the stairs." Duke yelled.

As they were running Kent realized something, why is nobody in the building?

"Hey, guys, why is nobody here?"

"I'm not sure, but it couldn't be too ba- It's an implosion!"

"How do you know?" Rose asked.

"Well I've never seen a building empty and have caution tape around it without being imploded."

"Good point, let's just get to the roof." When they got to the top of the building and looked on one side, no aliens were climbing up, the aliens were hiding from the demolition workers.

"If we run down to the bottom, and get out that way, we could escape."

"What if the aliens are inside the building?" said Duke.

"I think people will help us."

"We can't keep on running away! this is about Earth, not about us." Duke said, when they heard helicopter blades spinning near them.

"I always have a plan." Liam said.

"Liam?!" Rose said, feeling confused and happy. "But you died! You didn't have a heartbeat!"

"No way I would die." Liam said as they hopped in the helicopter.

"Quick, don't let the aliens grab on!" They started flying, Rose looked back and couldn't see much, but she knew the aliens didn't get on. "Where should we go?" Duke asked. "Why don't we follow that ship, it's the presidents!" Liam suggested. "Set Course!" Rose said. "To follow that airbus." As they were traveling, they felt turbulence.

"Watch out guys." Liam said. "It will be bumpy."

Rose went over and closed the cockpit door. "Guys, isn't Liam acting weird?" She said in a whispery voice.

"We don't know, we've never met the guy." Kent said. "I know he's an idiot." Said Kent.

 "Why do you hate him? OHH!" Duke said.

"What?" Rose asked.

"Nothing." He responded, trying to look casual.

"Ok?" Rose said. Rose sat down and put in some earbuds.

"While we're waiting, let's have some fun." Duke said turning on his phone and starting to play some music while grabbing some whiskey.

"Who's ready to party?!" Kent screamed. "Want a drink?" Kent asked Rose.

"I don't drink alcohol." She answered.

"Oh come on. You only live once." He said.

"Fine." She said grabbing some champagne. She was about to take a sip when the left door window broke open.

"Are we okay Liam?" Duke asked, opening the door to the cockpit.

"Grab this." Liam said handing him a parachute bag, and bringing three more.

"Kent, Rose, we gotta go." They opened the door and looked at the back of the plane. There were aliens. One crawled through the window. "Jump Now!" Liam said.

They jumped. "What's happening?!" Duke yelled as they looked and saw that Liam was chained to Duke who was chained to Rose who was chained to Kent who was getting held back by an alien.

"Kent! Punch the alien!" said Rose.

Kent punched it and they started going. But an alien on the back caught them. "Wait, the aliens are melting onto the plane."

"Metal kills them." Liam said.

"How did you know that?" Kent asked him.

"Trust me, I wish I didn't." Liam said, pushing the aliens head into the metal of the plane. Liam saw that the aliens were taking over the plane as him and Kent put up their parachutes, while Rose and Duke were chained to them.

"I've got to get to the president." Liam said.

"Why?" Kent asked.

"Because, if they take the plane to the presidents, then he could be in trouble." answered Liam. They got to the ground when the aliens tried to hit the president's ship with some missiles, luckily, they missed. They also saw a Space Agency ship from the left flow over with the aliens.

"Umm, guys, what's that thing?" Kent asked.

"It's getting closer!" Duke added.

"OH MY GOD! IT'S ON FIRE! IT'S A PART OF THAT PLANE! RUN!" Rose yelled.

Part IV

The Explanation

August 30th, 2095

"Help! Please! NO! NO! You're too late! It's coming!"

Diago said, trying to hook up his big circular phone looking

thing.

BBBZZZZ!

"Wait! Can you read me!" BUUZ YEZzBS

"YES!"

"Oh you can hear me. Look, I got the Hironafriom. Just

bring me backup to get out."

"BZZB We're coming BZcB"

"Oh NO! The tide is coming through. You'll never make i-"

"Diago! No! BZZNB"

"The mic is off, we didn't get in time. I hope Conner

knows what to do. Because if he doesn't, it seems the

whole Earth will pay for our mistakes."

5 days later…

"Hello, this is local news. See that big black dot in the sky,

yeah, that's an asteroid. I'm in the Southern Ocean and

there is only one year before supposedly an asteroid a

third of the size of the one that the dinosaurs got hit with

will hit us. Oh I just got an update from Lee Kentlint, and

Tyson Ofender, who are these people? OH MY GOD! The

message said, we've got, maybe 10 minutes before that

massive asteroid hits the ground. Kevin, Go, Go, G-"

BZZZZZZZZZZ.

"Gracen, did you see that!" Vicky asked Gracen.

"You mean that fake stuff they put on Tv." Gracen responded.

"No, I mean Hetamont live." Vicky said.

"WHAT!" Gracen said, standing corrected.

"Ya, by the way I still bought the special devices, the ones that save you, sort of." Vicky said.

"Thank goodness." Gracen said, sighing in relief. He took one and gave one to Vicky, and kept one for himself.

"Ya know, since you own Steel Engine maybe you could-" Vicky got cut off by Gracen.

"Vicky, look!" They both saw their lives flash in front of themselves, and so, what looked like an entire ocean.

2 years later...

"Vicky, come on. Get up."

"Ok, I'm up." Vicky said.

"Haha! Your car actually survived." Vicky said.

"Steel Engine creates the best cars." Gracen advertises.

"Gracen, is that a Navy Submarine, on land!?"

"Well, those few hours we were out, a lot happened."

"Umm, sir, I think our devices are broken, they say that

it's December 14th, 2097." They walked out of the garage.

"What the heck is that thing?" Gracen said, looking at the

large bulb in the sky.

"It's the sun."

"Let's drive over to Santopalie and see what's happening."

They pulled up to where Santopalie Studios was.

"Oh my god."

"It's just water and dust." Vicky said.

"Let's go to Houston." Gracen said.

"What!?" Vicky asked.

"Let's go to Houston and ask . You've got your pilots

licence." "Sir I'm sorry but, like-" Gracen cut her off.

"The private jet's fueled up from last time, and I'm sure

Jerome got a device, we'll just call him, and you'll be the

co-pilot."

"Yes sir." Vicky said, with worry. They got home, and

made the call.

"Hey, Jerry, we were wondering if you, well, first of all,

thank goodness you're alive, anyways, could you come to

Gracen's house and fly us to Houston?"

"Sir, but Vicky, you know I'm only in it for the money, is he

still paying us the bonus?"

"Don't worry, I know Gracen, he will do that for us."

"Good, I'm coming." When Jerome arrived, they got in the

plane. Jerome picked up the captain's mic.

"You buckled up, because we are."

Gracen picked up his mic,

"You can take off." He said, taking a sip of white wine.

3 hours later.

"Ahh, I haven't been to the rodeo state in a while."

Gracen said getting off the plane.

"Well then, Let's take the car out of the cargo place and

get to the Lost Pollen Hotel." They stayed the night and

left in the morning. He went to the hotel room next to

him and knocked on the door.

"Vicky. Time to go." She came out of her room.

"Let's head to the Space Agency sir."

"Hey, Elizabeth? Who's the guy with the fancy sports car

out front?" said George.

"I'm not sure, let's go check it out." answered Elizabeth.

They went in the elevator and went to the first floor.

"Hello, I'm Gracen, Gracen Airborne. This is my assistant

Vicky Davis, we were wondering what the heck

happened?" "We have some video of William Anderson,

come over here and we will show it."

"I'm coming." They went in and watched the

documentary. The scientists then took them to the top

floor.

"Wait, does that mean that everyone in other continents

is all dead?" Gracen asked, wanting to throw up.

"No, no," The scientists responded.

"They could have gotten the special devices you got too."

"What about poor people?" asked Gracen.

"We donated millions of the devices to every tribe,

homeless shelter, and we even asked thousands of

volunteers to go to some of the places, and give them out

to people that were poor." answered Elizabeth.

"But when the devices wake them up, then what?"

"These micro bots were designed to hibernate you until it

is safe." said Elizabeth.

"How do they work?" Gracen asked, very confused on this

whole thing.

"Well I didn't design them, but I know it gets fueled by

solar energy to keep you warm, and it stores up energy

for the night, and it can use your own body to feed water

into you, I'm not too sure about the food part, and it

creates blood and cells, like a organ, so if you were getting

pushed into a building, then it controls you and makes

you dodge it."

"What about people piloting planes, when their device turns on, they go to sleep, leaving all the passengers to be in danger." Gracen replies.

"The devices hack whatever technology you're using and pilot it safely." answered Elizabeth.

 "Well, I guess you thought of everything. Except what about when we get too close to the sun!"

"Oh, do you mind going to NYC?" asked Elizabeth.

"Me, no, Vicky do you mind?" answered Gracen.

"Sir I'm fine with anything," said Vicky.

"Where's the plane at?" Gracen asked.

"Follow me." said Elizabeth. They all went to a massive garage with planes everywhere.

"Which one are we taking?" Gracen asked.

"This beauty." Elizabeth said, climbing in.

"You know, this thing was built last year, but it's supposed to live for a thousand years." They took off.

"Well, If my ears don't fall off after all these plane rides I should get a prize." Gracen exclaimed humorously.

Vicky came into the room with a large plate, it had a salad, almonds and pretzels in a bowl, and a big ham sandwich. She also had a cup of chai tea. "Mmm! I'm starving. Thank you Vicky." He said taking the plate. "How much longer until we're there?" Gracen asked Vicky.

"About 10 minutes."

"Since the documentary said it had been two years, am I 24, or am I still 22?"

"Not sure sir."

"Please stay buckled up because we're landing."

"Five minutes left sir." said Vicky.

"You know, when we are all done with this, I should make a movie based on it." exclaimed Gracen.

"Sir, do you want to completely switch jobs?" asked Vicky.

"Well, If you're a 24 year old person who can already retire you can do anything you want." said Gracen.

"Ok sir." Vicky said.

"I can already imagine it, one of the scientists would obviously be played by Alan Collon. And I'll be played by Christopher Sapphire." Gracen said.

"It's your money sir." Said Vicky.

"It will be perfect Vicky, You'll be played by someone too, so you'll be famous as well." Gracen said.

"Thank you sir." Vicky said. They landed and got off the plane.

"AW MAN!" Gracen said looking at the massive ship with a E and a B connected on the bottom.

"What does it do?" Gracen asked Elizabeth.

"See, the engine that's attached doesn't create pollution, so, were pretty much gonna turn the Earth around so the meteor pushes the Earth the other way."

"Hmm, and if that would work why wouldn't it go the other way at night?"

"The atmosphere doesn't spin, why would the mass of it?" "Good point as well, except that how can you turn the atmosphere around?"

"You'll see." She said. "Oh, well can I be the one to push the button?" Gracen asked. "Ya, that's the thing, in order for it to work we can't be on Earth." Elizabeth said.

"So." Gracen said. "It's not like actually ever going outside of the rocket, I wouldn't need training."

"I'm sorry sir, but we'll use a professional, and we still don't have enough funds." said Elizabeth.

"How about I pay you what you need, and I get to hit the button." asked Gracen.

"Can you please just give us the money, you know it's not safe for you to go on the ship."

"Well, only if you had the money."

"I'll take you to Mr. McDaniels." Elizabeth said, with hints of sorrow. They got to his office.

"So, we get the money, you get the ride." Mr. McDaniels said, with a slight Irish accent. "Perfect, how much do you need?" Gracen said.

"300 million more." said Mr. McDaniels.

"Cash or Cheque?" Gracen asked him.

"That's a joke, right? You're actually going to send an E-transfer." Mr. McDaniels said.

"Cheque it is." Gracen said, giving him his piece of paper.

"Wow! You're rich." Mr. McDaniels said. "Even richer than

me, and I worked hard to get this far." Mr. McDaniel said in a suspicious voice.

"When do I go on the ship?" Gracen asked Elizabeth when they were driving to the hotel.

"You mean into space, in about two days." She answered.

"Who else is coming?" He asked her.

"A missionary, a scientist, and a pilot. Maybe more." She said. They got to the Pinihah Hotel. "So, what is the ship called?" Gracen asked her as they got out of the car.

"Mr. McDaniels just calls it, The EB, I could ask him what it means though. You see, Mr. McDaniels has a, creative brain. His idea for the name is probably what you may call, creativity in disguise. He didn't have a delightful past, his two best friends disappeared one day when the EB was almost finished, and they never came back." said Elizabeth.

"Hmm, well then." Gracen said. "We're going to JFK Airport in the morning."

"Yay, more plane riding."

"Haha, get some sleep Mr. Airborne." said Elizabeth.

Gracen went to his hotel room, and tried to get some sleep, but he could only think about one thing, what about if it's morning, and it was too late. What if everyones gone? For once in his life Gracen thought about something he'd never had before, others. He got out of bed, got out of the building, and got in his car and drove to the EB building. "Is anyone here?" He said, waiting for an answer.

"Aah. Mr. Airborne." Mr. McDaniels said to him.

"Hey, Mr. McDaniels."

"Gracen, please, call me Conner." said Mr. McDaniels.

"Ok, I was wondering if we could go to JFK Airport today."

"Sure, I'll drive us there," said Conner.

"You've got a pilot's license Conner?" Gracen asked him.

"No, but it can't be too hard to learn." Conner said, while

Gracen saw two empty beer bottles in Conner's hand and

two more on the ground.

"Conner you're drunk!" stated Gracen.

"I'm fine, now, I'll go start up the plane."

"Conner I'm gonna have to stop you."

"No!" Conner said, running out of the building, and

locking the backdoor as well.

"Conner! No!" Gracen said, trying to open the back door.

It wouldn't even budge. He ran to the front door. Conner

locked it too. He ran up the stairs and broke the window

so that Conner could hear him. "Conner! Stop!"

"See you at JFK, Gracen!" Conner replied. Gracen thought

if he jumped he may not die, but he won't be able to walk

for an hour. "It's not that high." He said to himself. "Oh boy." He said. And so, he jumped.

Conner saw him scream "AHH!" as he landed and the only sober part of his brain, made him stop and see if Gracen was ok. "I got you Gravy. Let's go get on the plane."

"What? NO! And my name is Gracen!" Gracen said, trying to get up and run. He couldn't. The only thing moving him, was what he thought would be the death of him. "Stop Conner! You can't fly." Gracen said, as Conner put him on a seat and strapped him in. Gracen could somewhat move his arms, and he grabbed his phone and called Elizabeth, who's car he saw pulling into the parking lot. He told her what was happening and saw her get out of the car, and ran over. She just made it up the step ladder and on the plane when it started moving slowly. "Well, I guess he found out how to start it." Gracen said, sounding surprised.

Elizabeth heard him and ran over. "You ok?" She said.

"I'm fine, go tell Conner to stop the plane." He said

"Why didn't you?" She asked.

"I tried, and it sprained both my ankles, now quickly go." He said.

She ran to the cockpit. "Conner, stop!" She said.

"Well, don't you look like a pretty little girl." He said back to her, after drinking another bottle already. She moved him aside and looked at the controls. "How do I stop this thing!?" She said.

"Aren't you a pilot!" Gracen said from way back in the seat. "Yes, but I can't stop it without the key!" She said back.

"Ok well, just fly to JFK and get us slow enough to jump out!" He said.

"JUMP OUT?!" She responded. "It's a fifty foot jump Gracen!" She said.

"Ya, but there will be a step ladder there too!" "We can't both jump with Mr. Beerman here and we would have to be very well timed!" said Elizabeth.

"Well ya, we'll never make it with that attitude. But if we slowly drive up to the roof of the airport it's plenty of time." said Gracen.

"I guess it's worth a try." She said, about to take off. "Here we go!" She said. Three minutes later they were back on the ground. "You ready Gracen?" Elizabeth said as they were coming up to the roof.

"Ready as ever." He said. They were next to the roof. First Elizabeth threw Conner on the roof. Then, with her help,

Gracen got up and jumped and sort of fell on the roof due to what happened when he was trying to stop Conner. Then Elizabeth finally jumped out right before the plane wasn't next to the building anymore. When they looked back they saw they lost a piece of their left engine way back near Central New York. Four people were running out of where the piece fell just before it hit the ground. "What are the chances, two of the people who are going on the ship, are two of those four people, oh, and there's the reason we came here, hey Mr. Mcdonald! Could you help us down?!" She asked him.

"What are you doing up there?!" Reagan said, grabbing a long ladder. "Here!" He said, putting down the ladder. Elizabeth came down, forgetting Gracen couldn't walk and Conners passed out.

"Hey! What about us?!" Gracen said.

"Oh ya, sorry." She said. "Mr. McDonald, could you help me get them down, and get a wheelchair?"

"I'm coming." Reagan said. After everyone was down and Gracen had crutches, The president was about to land, and so was the ship full of aliens, and the four people that almost got hit by the engine, got to the airport. Conner started to wake up. "Huh? What happened, the last thing I remember was, Gracen, Elizabeth, you saved me, wait, we made it to JFK?"

"Don't worry Mr. McDaniels, we have the four to go on the EB with us, and we just need to fly them back." said Elizabeth.

 "Wait, what are those black humanoid beings on that aircraft?" asked Reagan.

"What the heck are those?" Gracen said.

"I know what they are." Duke said, pulling out a tactical

handgun that had blue lights on the side, they made it

shoot extra hard. "Die you aliens." He said, pulling back

the trigger. He shot most of them, and the others died

from when he shot the gas tank. "Oh boy, that should be

the last of them." Duke said, with a grin on his face. "Ok,

everyone can fit on that plane, so get on!"

Part V

Test Run

"It's Insanity!! It's my evil queen!" Jackson sang off of the song he was listening to.

"Jackson, shut up! Nobody wants to hear your music, that's why dad gave you earbuds!" said Karen.

"Oh, well now I'll sing louder……..At the coward I've come to be!" Jackson screeched.

"That's it." Karen said, grabbing his ear and pulling on it.

"Ow! Oh that's it!" Jackson said, jumping onto his sister and spitting on her.

"Hey. Guys, stop fighting." Hue said, not trying to sound mean.

"Fine." Jackson said, getting off his sister.

"I get that it's boring, but we'll be taking off in about 5 minutes." Hue said. The president walked into the part of the plane they were in with his wife.

"I hope they didn't cause any trouble." The first lady said.

"They were fine." Hue said back and then he walked into another room, where there was Lily, Duke, Liam, Rose, Kent, Reagan, Sarah, Johny, and Hue's two dads.

"Hey everyone." Hue said.

"Hi." Lily, Sarah, Reagan, Rose, and his two dads said back.

"Daddy? Why are we in the tiny room with lots of people, but Mr. Airborne gets a massive room and it's only him, Elizabeth, Mr. McDaniels, and Ms. Davis?" Sarah asked her father.

"And where's mommy?" She asked again.

"Well, think about it this way, in this room, we get to have three astronauts, and they only get one."

"Oh, so we're bettew dan dem." Sarah said.

"Yup." Her step-dad said back.

"But still, where's mommy?" She asked again.

"She's in Vermont doing business. But she's still ok."

"Oh, I sure miss mommy." Sarah said. The plane started to take off. The speakercom on the plane turned on.

"Attention, we'll arrive at our destination in three minutes and fifty-five seconds. I hope you like Manhattan folks." The speaker turned off.

"Can I go speak with the president?" Liam questioned them.

"Do whatever you want." Kent answered. Liam opened the door.

"Hello Mr. President." Liam said.

"Hi, have we met?" The president asked Liam.

"Just once, you wouldn't recognize me now. I've changed alot since then, I was almost a kid. But it's still an honor to see you again."

"Pleasure to meet you too." The president said.

"You have an adorable son." Liam said, walking towards Jackson.

"Owch!" Jackson said, after Liam stepped on his foot.

"Sorry, clumsy me." Liam said.

"I'd better get back to my room now." Liam said, opening the door back to his room.

"Have a wonderful day, Mr. President." Liam said, exiting the room.

"You too." The president said back.

"What a weird guy." The first Lady said after he closed the door.

"Yeah." The president said. They landed down on the ground.

"After that twelve minutes it feels good to get fresh air." Gracen said.

"Oh, My, God!" Hue said, looking up at the massive rocket. "Is that 50 nuclear bombs merged into a massive rocket." Lily asked.

"I helped make it." Gracen said. A massive speaker turned on.

"Attention, can Kent Gathernton, Reagan McDonald, Gracen Airborne, and Liam Freshman all come to room eleven on the northwest tower strain.

"Where's that?" Gracen asked.

"Follow me." Conner said, the four going in the rocket followed him. Once they got up, there was a youngish lady waiting for them.

"Can each of you write your signature right here and here." She said holding out a piece of paper. They did what she told them to do.

"Thank you, now this is what we call training, just in case something wrong happens. I want you to jump off this tower." said the young lady.

"We'll die." Reagon said.

"Not if you put on these. See these watches, they are magnets, and you'll attach to the railing."

"They each put on the watch, and pressed the green button. "First, I want Kent to jump, then Liam, then Reagan, then Gracen." She said. Kent ran and jumped off, and he attached to the railing below them, then Liam jumped, but his watch wouldn't work. He was at the final floor of the tower when he attached to the railing before he hit the ground.

"Oh my gosh." She said. "He definitely broke his arm."

"I'm fine!" Liam yelled up to them.

"No, that would be impossible." The young lady said.

"Are you sure you're ok?!" She yelled down to him.

"Yup, I'm fine." Liam said, getting back on the tower and running back up the stairs.

"Well, that's odd." She said.

"Ok boys, follow me." She said taking them to a small weird room. It had a messy fake control panel.

"I'm going to show you how to work the thing, in case we lose contact with the ship."

About four hours later, they finally finished the instructions, and started walking to a smaller EB.

"We're gonna start a test run, everybody strap in." They did a couple of seat belts each, then all the doors shut, and they felt a strong quake and took off.

"Oh My God!" Said Kent in a wavy voice. They went around the station. The speaker inside of the ship turned on.

"You're going into the atmosphere now." The speaker turned off. They started getting higher and higher. They reached the atmosphere and the speaker turned on again.

"Undo your belts and try walking around." It turned off. They got up.

"Oh man, I've never had to hold onto the ground before." Liam said.

"Neither have I." Gracen said. The speakers turned on again. "Everyone strap in, we will be leaving in one minute and 15 seconds, 14 seconds, 13 seconds." The computer voice kept on counting down, they all got in and were ready to go, when oddly at one minute and nine seconds, the voice shut off, so did all the lights and the emergency strap didn't shoot out like it should've. "Hey, Liam what's going on? You're a scientist." Gracen asked

"I, I don't know." He said. They tried to fly back themselves but the controls on the weren't working. They were a small black dot in the abyss of space, without control of where they are headed.

Part VI

The Mothership.

"Is this it?" Kent said.

"I wish we had a window." Gracen said, unbuckling

himself. "Woah!" Reagan said,

"We're sure going fast for not going anywhere." Gracen

said.

"Were too far from Earth for it's gravitational flow to pull

us, we must be near something massive." Liam said.

PUUHTZ! They hit something.

"What happening, why's the door opening," Liam said.

"I guess we should get out." He said again, walking out of

the ship.

"At Least there's air on this rock, actually, it's more like a

shi- OH NO!" Kent said.

"I know where we are, there are these alien guys, and I think they took control of our ship." Kent said.

"Yes Kent, a whole bunch of aliens abducted us and we are on their ship, that doesn't sound insane or anything, I'm sure the things on that army plane were just a weird species or something." Gracen said, walking around the ship. "ZZDYKXHFYGYHGYJHFN MMDBC!" Something from above said.

"Of course, I stand corrected." Gracen said in a worried tone, running down a hallway with the others, the creatures following.

Back on Earth…

"I lost connection with the Mini EB, but I'll try restarting the system." Eizabeth said.

"Is daddy ok?" Johnny asked.

"Don't wuwwy Johnny, wouw daddy wiww be ok." Sarah said, hugging him.

"No! What the-"

"Hey, Elizabeth, there's kids, no profanity." Vicky said.

"Sorry, but it won't let me turn it back on, I'm gonna send a drone to get them." Elizabeth said.

"Wait, why is there a big dot right where they are?" Vicky said.

"What are you talking about? My computer doesn't show anything like that near them." Elizabeth said.

"Not on the computer, look out the window, what's that black dot?" Vicky asked while they were looking.

"It's a huge ship." Elizabeth answered.

Back on the Mini EB…

"Oh God! They're catching up to us." Reagan yelled.

"I'm gonna distract them, keep going." Liam said.

"No, Liam you can't." Gracen said.

"I don't care.'' Liam said, running back near the horde, then running down another hallway. The aliens followed him.

"I hope he doesn't die." Kent said.

"Let's get back to the ship, that's probably where he'd meet up with us." Gracen says, turning around, as the others followed him.

Back on Earth...

"I've got an idea, let's send a drone to get them." Hue said. "I'm sorry but there's no drone that won't turn into a roasted marshmallow when it reaches the atmosphere." Elizabeth said.

"I'll go, I've got a pilot's licence." Vicky stated.

"Normally I'd say no, but if Conner finds out about this

he'd kill me, so, let's get you on your ship." Elizabeth said.

 Back on the Mini EB...

They got back to the ship.

"Let's just hide here until, well let's just stay here." They

waited for hours and hours.

"What's left of this," Kent yelled.

"Am I gonna die on an alien ship a million miles away from

my house!?"

"Oh quit complaining Kent! I'm sure we'll make it out of

here. what's that light?" Gracen asked.

"It's getting closer!" Reagan said. The small light soon was

a ship, and it was next to them. Vicky hopped out of it and

told them to get in.

"Wait, there's Liam, wait for him!" Gracen said.

"But the aliens could get on." Kent replied.

"We have to wait for him." Gracen pleaded.

"Fine." Vicky said. Liam jumped into the ship and they took off before the aliens got on, leaving a detonable nuke on the ship.

"That'll kill most of them once it hit the gas tank." Vicky said.

"Actually, I don't think it had a gas tank." Liam said.

"Why don't we test that theory." Gracen said, setting off the detonator. Behind them was the massive explosion.

"Boss, did you even know if we were far enough away or not?" Vicky asked.

"I didn't know for sure, but we'll find out soon if we start vomiting." Gracen answered.

"Gas tank or not from the explosion I saw I know they're all dead." Reagon said. They made it back to Earth a couple hours later.

"We're back, everyone!" Kent screamed happily.

"Oh my god, after I heard what happened, I almost died," Rose said.

"Kent, I was wondering if we could go on a date? You know, after we save the Earth." Rose asked him.

"I'll pick you up at 6:30 this Saturday." Kent answered. The speaker came on.

"Kent Gathernton, Liam Freshman, Reagan McDonald, and Gracen Airborne, please meet me at zone 44." It turned off. "I'm guessing you'll need to follow me." Conner said. They walked into the building next to the EB.

"Were about to save the world." Gracen said.

"And we don't have a choice." Kent added when they were going up the stairs.

"But, we were born for this."

"Mr. McDaniel, what does EB stand for?" Gracen asked.

Mr. McDaniel replied, "Easter Blankets."

Part VI

Take Off.

"You guys ready?" Mr. McDaniel asked. "Yup." They all said. "And you're sure you want to go."

"Yup." They all said, climbing aboard the EB.

"Goodbye Earth!" Kent said. The youngish girl came running over to the control room. "STOP THE LAUNCH!"

"It's too late." The man in the control room said. The screen above started reading 5,4,3,2.

"NO!" She said as it took off. "There's a massive heat signature above, bigger than the ship from before, I think it's trying to stop the EB!" The young lady said.

"This isn't comfortable." Gracen said, laying almost upside down on the ship. The speaker on the ship turned on.

"Stop the ship! Stop the ship!" It cut out. Liam got out of his seat. "Liam, sit down, it's dangerous." Reagan said.

"The Earth turned its back on me. Now I'm gonna turn my back on it. You thought I was Liam, I'm the person you thought was DIZI, which you read upside down, it was IZIC, and a wrinkle added the line in the D." Liam said, as his skin peeled off, he turned into a strange mangled black creature, with skinny long fingers, and he was growing until he was eight feet tall.

"Liam?! What's wrong with you?!" Kent asked. "Liam, Izic, call me what you want, but soon you'll be decapitated, and the worlds gonna run into the sun, and I'm gonna be sitting with millions of creatures by my side laughing."

"Your plan will never work Liam."

"That's where you're wrong, see that ship up there, it's one of the thousands across the solar system, waiting for my order to kill all of you." stated Liam.

"Well, but, ya were done for." Gracen said.

"Not if we can make it into space in time."

"Oh." Alien creature Liam said, pulling out a weird phone gadget thing. "IOIGIOKGLVJYI!" He said into it.

"What does that mean?" Gracen asked.

"I told my friends to kill you three." Liam said turning around to turn the ship in the direction of his ship above.

"NO!" Kent said, pushing him aside.

"Kent, I know you've hated me since we met, and that's why I'm about to kill you with my own two hands."Liam remarked fiercely. Reagan jumped and pushed Liam farther back near one of the big windows. "I know what I've got to do." Kent said. The radio turned back on.

"Guys? Guys?" Gracen grabbed the mic. "We're here. Except Liam is an alien, but Reagan and Kent are fighting him." he said.

"Gracen, tell Rose I love her. I'm gonna take Liam out with me." Kent said.

Rose heard him off the mic. "No! Kent you can't." Rose said. "Don't do it Kent!" Duke said.

"Like you said Captain, this is about Earth, not about us." Kent said, as he ran, grabbed Liam, and jumped out the window entangled with Liam. Reagan pressed a button to put a metal shield around the window to cover the broken opening.

"He did it. He jumped." Gracen said into the mic.

"Gracen, Look Out!" Reagan said. They almost hit the massive ship, but Reagan turned them in time.

"What happened?" Duke asked from the speaker com.

"It's ok, we're fine." Reagan said.

"No we're not." Gracen said looking out a window at the hundreds of aliens climbing the ship. "Let's drop the engine now." Gracen said.

"Gracen, when I hit the emergency button, anybody in any room gets closed in when they walk in, and after they hit the button, with the ventilation off, as soon as the door closes it'll trap them and the Easter Blankets will float away, with them locked inside." Reagan explained to him.

"Well then, Vicky, I hope Steel Engines is safe in your hands. And I hope the charities and fundraisers are happy that I'm giving them my bank account." Gracen said into the mic, running into the room as the door closed on him. He hit the button, and dropped the engine, knowing he'd be trapped, and soon, launched thousands of miles away, where he'd lay there and die, never to know love, never

to know friendship, but at least he died with one thing. He

died knowing he did one good thing.

Part VIII

A Happy Ever After?

"The aliens are gonna get on the ship. My team is all dead or thousands of miles away. What do I do?" Reagan said into the mic.

"I have a professional here, his name is George, he thinks he can get the ship back." Elizabeth said.

"I sure hope he can, because if he can't, I'm dead." Reagan said. The aliens broke in through a window down the hallway. "They are in, it's too late." Reagan said, running away from them. He locked himself in a room, pulling out a knife. He unlocked the door and ran out. They were almost there, he held out the knife, and when they got there, he fought for his life. One of the aliens scratched him.

"If I'm gonna die, you're going down with me." Reagan said. There were six massive ships with the first one, all full of aliens. Reagan got through some of the aliens and turned the EB to run into all the alien ships, and he ran to the escape pods. Oddly, the first two were locked, he got to the third one, ran inside and locked the door and shot himself into the crowd of alien ships, with a detonatable nuke in his hand. "Goodbye you little-" BOOOOM!!! Most of the six ships were blown up, and the other will get destroyed when the Easter Blankets runs into them. "I think he's dead." Vicky said. "Whaw's daddy?" Johnny asked.

"I'm right here." Reagan said, walking away from a crashed escape pod. "I threw in the nuke, then when I got out of Earth's atmosphere, since I was far enough away, I hit the button. But why is the EB turning? It's going away from Earth."

"Daddy!" Johnny said running over to him.

"Is there a Mrs. McDonald?" Vicky asked.

"No, and I'll pick you up at seven." Reagan said.

"Well then, after we finish off killing the other alien ships, I guess it was a happy ever after." Lily said.

"Ya, we made some horrible sacrifices, but in the end, we did good. Lily, I was wondering if you'd like to go to the cinema sometime, like, together." Hue said.

"Ok, sure." Lily said, with a smile on her face.

"Hey, Elizabeth?" George said.

"Yeah?" She said coming over to him.

"There seems to be an oddly big heat signature right out of our solar system, and it's getting bigger. I'm starting up the phone with the Space Agency." George said.

"That's weird." Elizabeth said.

"What the heck!?" George yelled.

"What?" Elizabeth asked.

"Jupiter is starting to move out of its solar course."

"No way! Let me see that. What, your right!" She said.

George picked up a microphone to the left of him. "Space Agency! Space Agency! Space Agency! Do you copy?" George said into the microphone. "We can hear you." They said back. "Ok, umm, Agency, I think we've got ourselves a black hole!"